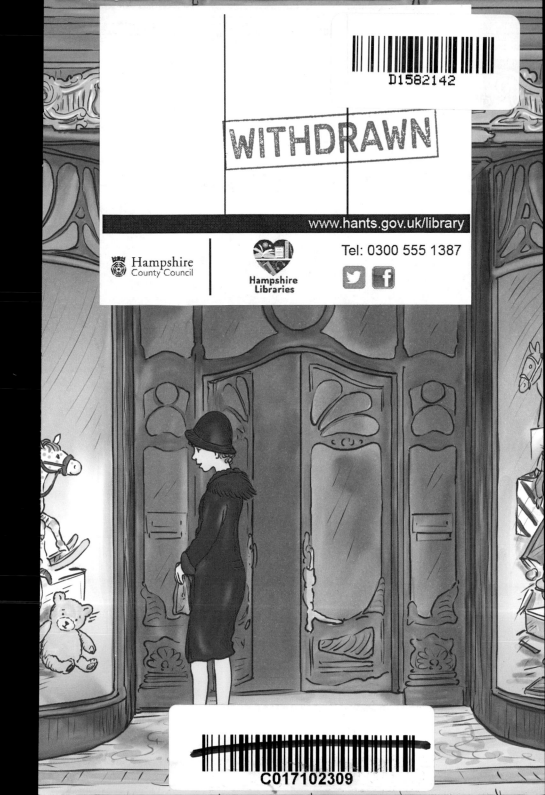

Once
There
Was a
Bear

Farshore

First published in Great Britain 2021 by Farshore
An imprint of HarperCollins*Publishers*
1 London Bridge Street, London SE1 9GF
www.farshore.co.uk

HarperCollins*Publishers*
1st Floor, Watermarque Building, Ringsend Road,
Dublin 4, Ireland

Edited by Catherine Shoolbred
Designed by Pritty Ramjee

With special thanks to Nicole Pearson and Rebecca Oku

Text by Jane Riordan copyright © 2021 The Trustees of the Pooh Properties and the Estate of E.H.Shepard
Illustrations by Mark Burgess copyright © 2021 The Trustees of the Pooh Properties and the Estate of E.H.Shepard

An Authorised Prequel to A.A.Milne's Original Winnie-the-Pooh Stories,
written by Jane Riordan in the style of A.A.Milne, and illustrated by
Mark Burgess in the style of the Original E.H.Shepard decorations.

A CIP catalogue record for this title is available from the British Library.

ISBN 978 0 7555 0073 4
Printed in Great Britain by Bell and Bain Ltd, Glasgow
005

Farshore takes its responsibility to the planet and its inhabitants very seriously.
We aim to use papers from well-managed forests run by responsible suppliers.

Once There Was a Bear

Tales of Before it all Began...

Jane Riordan
with decorations by Mark Burgess
Inspired by A.A.Milne and E.H.Shepard

Farshore

BEFORE THE BEFORE
(AN INTRODUCTION)

Writing is a tricky thing. Sometimes the words are so comfortable in your head that they refuse to come out for days and days and, even when they do, they grumble, and they jostle crossly on the page and they simply will not sit nicely next to their neighbours. On other days, they're as happy as can be and skip along faster than you can write them down.

When I was lucky enough to be asked to write about Before Christopher Robin lived in a tree in the Hundred Acre Wood, Before Eeyore had a birthday and Before Piglet did a Very Grand Thing, most of the words behaved very nicely and did as they were told. But then a clever person at the place where books are made said, 'What about the Introduction?'

'The what?' said I, pretending I hadn't heard because I was terribly busy that day trying to do nothing at all. 'The Introduction,' they said again, 'we always have one of those. Mr Milne did and so should you.' Now Mr Milne sadly died when I would have been about minus twenty years old, but of all the writers in the world he is the one I most like to listen to and so if Mr Milne says that's how it is, then that's how it is, and *here it is*.

Pooh says it's not very long. Eeyore says he stopped listening at about the part when the words were skipping and that it's far *too* long. But if Pooh is right, and he often is, then I'm not worried because I know that the talented Mr Burgess will draw a perfect picture, just like Mr Shepard taught him, and that will help to fill up the space.

You may also want to scatter a few crumbs over the page, because a book is generally best enjoyed with a little nibble of something (or so Pooh says).

J.R.

For Isaac, Oscar, Hannah
and Alice – the den builders

J.R.

ACKNOWLEDGMENTS

With acknowledgments to A.A.Milne,
author of the original Winnie-the-Pooh stories
and E.H.Shepard, who illustrated them.

The publisher would like to thank
the Trustees of the Pooh Properties and the Shepard Trust,
whose knowledge shared and suggestions made during
the creation of this book have been invaluable. Also,
Stephanie Thwaites and Isobel Gahan of Curtis Brown,
who helped to make it all possible.

CONTENTS

CHAPTER ONE

in which we go back to the beginnings

NOT SO VERY FAR AWAY THERE IS A FOREST. You've
probably been there. It's the sort of Forest with
trees to hide behind, sticks to bend and snap, streams to
wet your toes in and steep running down-y bits to run
down. In this Forest, two friends sat in a patch of sunlight.

'There isn't a cloud in the sky,' announced Christopher
Robin as he leaned his head right back, until Pooh Bear
(Winnie-the-Pooh to some and just Pooh to you and me)
was worried it might fall off.

'I wonder where they all are,' mused Pooh.

'Who?' asked Christopher Robin.

'The clouds,' replied Pooh.

'Oh,' said Christopher Robin, sleepily. It was a Very
Good Wonder for the month was April and the day was
possibly a Tuesday or perhaps a Thursday, and really
there should have been April showers. Instead, there
was a glorious blue sky that stretched from the Floody
Place all the way to the North Pole, without the slightest
disturbance from a cloud, not even one of those shy wispy

ones who aren't quite sure if they should stay or go.

Christopher Robin and Winnie-the-Pooh were doing what they liked best. That is to say, not very much at all, but they were doing it together which made it a Thing To Do. This comfortable feeling of doing nothing much made Pooh Hum-ish. Today's hum went like this:

In winter, it is cold a lot.
In summer, it is not – it's hot.
In autumn, trees drop all their leaves-es.
In spring, the weather does whatever it pleases.

Here Pooh hesitated, for he had never quite sorted out the difference between spring and autumn and which is squeezed before summer and which hurries after it. He tried to untangle them but, much like Tuesday and Thursday, they seemed to change places when you weren't looking. Christopher Robin didn't correct him, so he hoped he'd got it right and continued:

But whatever the weather, whether windy or wet ...

Pooh wasn't able to finish his hum because something had very nearly landed on him.

'Hallo, Tigger,' said Christopher Robin, helping Pooh to get up again and brushing him down.

'Tiggers like games,' said Tigger with a large smile. 'What game is this?'

'It isn't,' said Pooh, a little put out, 'at least, it wasn't. It was a hum.'

'Oh,' said Tigger, who couldn't quite remember if a hum was something to eat or something to sit on. 'Tiggers like those, too.'

'Are you sure?' asked Pooh, 'Because when you arrived in the Forest you said you liked a great many things like honey, and I forget what else. But you didn't like any of them.'

And it was a funny thing, but as Pooh said the word "arrived", lots of friends did. That is to say, suddenly Piglet was there and Owl and then Kanga and little Roo and Rabbit of course, and wherever Rabbit went there were sure to be a whole host of friends and relations. Suddenly there was quite a crowd. Even Eeyore, who was often not there, was there.

'I'd forgotten all about arriving,' said Tigger, thoughtful for a moment. 'That was fun. Tiggers do like arriving. When I arrived there were lots of "hallos" and new friends to show my bouncing to, I mean to meet,' he corrected himself. 'How did you arrive, Christopher Robin?' he asked, excitedly.

'In the Forest?' asked Christopher Robin, a little surprised by the question. 'Oh, I've always been here.'

At this, Rabbit stepped forward. 'But there must be a Before,' he said, taking charge. 'There's always a Before.'

Christopher Robin didn't think there was, well not for him at any rate.

'Before,' said Owl, gravely, 'not to be confused with Aforetime or Hitherfore, is a Fact. That is to say that it is

Actual and Real. You should find out about your Before, Christopher Robin, and then tell it to us all.'

'Oh, like a story?' squeaked Roo, very much excited.

Kanga looked on proudly. 'Yes, Roo dear, you like your stories don't you. It isn't everyone who could sit so still and listen for so long,' she announced to the others. 'Well, just the other day ...' But they had already stopped listening.

Tigger was looking worried. And his worry was that Christopher Robin's Before wouldn't have any Tiggers in it.

'I like this story best,' he said, 'because I'm in it.'

'But *this* isn't a story,' said Christopher Robin, laughing. 'I can tell that because nothing much is happening.'

'Oh,' said Tigger, a little disappointed, but this didn't last long, for Tiggers always have bright ideas. 'I'll make something happen and then it'll be a story.' And with that he bounded off.

The others waited a little anxiously. Generally, when Tigger was around, things happened whether you wanted them to or not. But for a long while nothing happened at all and the friends went back to staring up at the clear blue sky and Pooh tried to remember where he had got to with his hum.

'I hate to be the one to dampen the mood,' said Eeyore, breaking the silence. 'But Tigger has been gone now for Some Time. Which isn't like him. In my experience,' and here he sighed, 'he's ALWAYS there. Here that is. Here and There, at any rate, and ALWAYS LOUD.' Eeyore's "always loud" was itself rather on the not-quiet-side and several of the smaller friends and relations jumped anxiously when he spoke. 'That is to say,' continued Eeyore, 'that it being so quiet makes me wonder where he is.'

Christopher Robin was much impressed by this speech. He knew that Eeyore and Tigger had not always been the best of friends. There was that business about the wetting in the river, from which Eeyore had never quite recovered …

'Eeyore,' said Christopher Robin, gravely. 'You have said a Very Kind Thing.' And at this Eeyore lowered his head and anyone who had peeped under one of his long, dangly ears, might have seen a slight blush. 'Tigger has been far too quiet, and we must find him.'

And so, they set off.

Rabbit would have liked to be the one who found Tigger. And Pooh was sure that he would have found him, if only he hadn't gone home for a little taste of honey. But it was, in fact, little Piglet who found him, and quite by accident.

Piglet had started the search in the best possible way … by searching. But after a while, what with the sun being so warm and the new leaves such a fresh bright green, he turned his little pink face up to the treetops and rather forgot about the search altogether. It was only when he tripped over something and landed face down in the Sandy Place, and his surprised cry brought everyone else running, that Christopher Robin noticed that the thing that Piglet had tripped over was stripy and tail-ish.

After that, there was pulling and when the pulling didn't work there was digging. Lots and lots of digging. Everyone helped. Of all the diggers, Roo was the most enthusiastic.

'Look at me! Look how I dig,' he called to whoever would listen. 'I'm the best, fastest digger of all.'

At last Tigger was dug out. He had swallowed a great deal of sand, which meant he was a little unclear about how his tail came to be in the sun and the rest of him in the sand.

'Worraw splah? Worraw spliph?' he spluttered. And then more clearly, 'Is this a story?'

'That's one way of putting it,' said Eeyore. 'If story and accident are the same. If story and calamity are the same. If story means filling your ears with sand.' And with this, Eeyore rather awkwardly raised a hoof and flapped at his ear, which dislodged enough sand to turn one of the smaller friends and relations – a mouse by the name of Gerald – into a sandmouse, if there is such a thing.

'Eeyore says it's a story!' continued Tigger, bouncing now in excitement. 'What do you say Christopher Robin?'

'Well,' said Christopher Robin, feeling very wise. 'I've been told that stories should have a beginning, a middle and an end.'

'Ha!' snorted Eeyore, with rather too much sand still in his ears. 'A muddle. Well yes, that says it all.'

'A middle, I think,' said Christopher Robin. 'Or perhaps it was a muddle. I forget. Anyway, this one had both. There was a beginning where Pooh and I were doing nothing much, and then a muddly middle with bouncing in it and searching and then an end with lots of sand. So, yes, I think this is a story.'

Tigger beamed with contentment and did a few big bounces to show how pleased he was.

'Now that Tiggers are in this story,' he said. 'I won't mind so very much if they're not in the Before ones.' And away he went with a

BOUN^{CE}! BOUN^{CE}! BOUN^{CE}!

* * *

And that is how Christopher Robin came to go home that evening with sand in his hair and sand in his socks, which meant an extra-long bath. And a bath, as you may well know, is not very much about washing, but a great deal about playing and story-telling. And so, as

Christopher Robin balanced bubbles on his nose and then blew them off again, he asked about the time long, long ago Before he had come to the Forest. Before he even knew Winnie-the-Pooh, if such a Before existed and certainly Before Christopher Robin was old enough to have given Pooh his name.

It was agreed that the stories would be told and Pooh would always be called Pooh in them, because without a name he wouldn't feel like he was really there.

And these are those stories …

CHAPTER TWO

in which a bear is bought

O NCE THERE WAS A BEAR ...

'Once upon a time?' asked Christopher Robin.

Once upon a time there was a bear sat on a shelf in a very grand department store called Harrods. There were, in fact, many bears. There were large bears with rough fur and cross faces. There were very small barely-there bears with arms that stuck stiffly out in front of them, as if they were worried about bumping into walls. And there were medium-sized bears with a faraway look in their eyes, that made you think that perhaps they were lost.

But among all of these bears, there was only one who really matters to us. He was no bigger or cleverer than the other bears, but he was OUR bear. Had he realised this, he might have felt a little more perky, but he didn't yet know his own name, or where he was or what was to become of him and, above all, on that particular day, he was Hungry. His generous and rounded tummy was beginning to rumble ... And rumbling was not allowed in that place, as another bear was quick to tell him.

'Rumbling is Not Allowed in this place,' said a not-bare bear wearing a green bellboy hat that looked in danger of slipping off his head, and a smart green jacket to match.

'Oh,' said our bear, Pooh Bear, a little surprised. 'I do try to tell my Grumbles not to become Rumbles, but they're not very good at listening, that is to say …'

'Talking is Not Allowed in this place,' continued the bear. 'It's a shop rule.'

Pooh wondered if the other bear had broken the rule to tell him the rule, but he was too polite to say so. He also thought that perhaps the bear who loved rules so much was cross because his tight-fitting jacket squeezed all the smile out of him and Pooh felt suddenly lucky to have a rounded … that is to say … generous … tummy. In any case, to have something that he could comfortably rest his paws upon.

But Pooh's thoughts were interrupted by a sound. It was the sort of sound that made your ears want to be somewhere else.

'Oh, look at that funny bear,' shouted a little girl in a puffy white dress that stuck out like a sugary meringue. 'He's all tummy with hardly any legs,' she laughed to herself, 'such a silly bear.'

But before Pooh had the chance to respond, she grabbed him down from the shelf and said, 'I Want him!' and since whoever her grown-up was didn't disagree, she marched off dragging poor Pooh behind her.

And so, it was in this very BUMP, BUMP, OWW, BUMP, BUMP, OUCH on the hard floor kind of a way, that Pooh saw a lot more of that grand shop than he had planned to.

And he soon learnt that the little girl who made his ears hurt wanted a great deal more than just a new bear. She wanted a colourful singing box with a handle that turned and a clown that jumped out when you least expected it. She also wanted a beautiful doll who closed her eyes when you laid her down and a wooden boat on wheels that had a little wooden door that opened and animals of every type that fitted inside it, always two of each.

'I Want it!' she would say, stamping her feet. And when there was no more stamp left in her shoes she stopped and said, 'I'm going sploring.'

Pooh hoped that this sploring, whatever that might be, would have less bump and ouch in it, but that wasn't to be …

'The bottom step should have stayed where it was,' Pooh thought to himself, as they were carried up a magical moving mountain for the fourth time in a row. 'Now the bottom part is at the top and there's more bottom at the bottom. I wonder where all that bottom comes from?'

'I Want one,' said the little girl, but the escalator, for that was what it was, didn't seem to be for sale.

In the food hall she was even worse …

'Did somebody say "food"?' asked Pooh. 'Because after all that bottom to top-ing my middle could do with being topped up, too.'

And what a sight the food hall was. Along every wall and down the centre of the room ran counters piled high with everything you could possibly imagine eating, and some things you had never thought to eat before, but would very much like to try.

The little girl was so busy pointing out to a very tired-looking shop assistant exactly which chocolates she had to have, that she let Pooh's paw slip and he tumble-bumped to the floor.

'No, not that one, I want the one with pink petals on it! And the one with strawberry cream!' And so it went on, until the enormous golden box looked like it might burst and the little girl walked away with it, sticky finger licking as she went.

There Pooh lay, downside up and upside down in a corner. He could just make out the pyramids of bright jellies in all the colours of the rainbow and next to them towers of miniature fruits, which were in fact not fruit at all, but coloured marzipan shaped into tiny, perfect bananas, oranges and rosy apples. To Pooh all of these were the other way up, so each pyramid seemed to balance on its sugary point and all the time the smell of lemon, violet and cinnamon-scented sweetness danced around Pooh's nose until he was quite dizzy with it all.

'A hum,' thought Pooh, as thoughtfully as he could manage in the circumstances, 'sung in a song-ish way is sure to help.' And this is what he sang:

When down is up and up is down,
It's funny to think that a smile is a frown.

So, if you're feeling glum for a while,
Stand on your head and your frown is a smile.

Pooh hummed this to himself several times over and practised the smiles and frowns until he wasn't sure which was which. But he could tell that it was getting late, from the way the footsteps around him stepped less often and the shop assistants began to laugh and tease each other, forgetting to stay serious now that it was nearly closing time.

'It's an odd thing,' he said to himself, 'how much that little girl looked like a sweet. Perhaps it was because she had eaten so many. Or perhaps not. Bees eat a good deal of honey, but they don't look like honey.' And then he drifted into a pleasant daydream filled with honey-coloured bees and buzzing sweets that flew out from behind the shop counters and fluttered all around the walls.

'When it gets dark,' said Pooh, dreamily, 'I generally like to get comfortable and this shiny-floored, downside-up place isn't what you'd call Comfortable.' But, at that moment, a gentle hand reached down and picked Pooh up. A young woman looked him up and down, kindly.

'Whatever is a young bear doing here?' she said to herself, smiling. 'Perhaps he likes all the sweet things?' Then she saw that he still wore his shop label and she decided at once to buy him, as there was someone waiting at home who would be sure to love him.

And so it was that Winnie-the-Pooh didn't go to live with the sugared-meringue girl who got everything she wanted (except once, when her love of sugar meant she let go of The Best Bear in All the World), but instead, Pooh was given as a present to a little boy who shared every secret with that bear and took him on all his Very Best Adventures.

* * *

'That's me!' said Christopher Robin, his eyes as big as the lollipops in the shop. 'If that little girl had kept Pooh, his fur would have been all stuck together with sticky sweets,' he mused, 'and there would be so many toys – piled right up to the ceiling – that Pooh would never be played with at all.' He also imagined Piglet without Pooh ... which was a Hard Thing To Do because it was unimaginable.

'Are there more Before stories?' asked Christopher Robin, hoping that the answer would be a Happy one. And when he heard that there were, he rested his chin on Pooh's head and thought how pleased he was that Pooh was all tummy and no legs and how he would never have called Pooh silly ... even if he was a tiny bit.

Chapter Three

in which some friends arrive

O N THE COLD DAY THE PARCEL WAS DELIVERED, Winnie-the-Pooh had been sitting in one of his favourite places in the nursery, gazing down at the street. The noise below floated up to his cushioned seat by the window.

'Do you think I've got all day to wait out here in this weather?' fumed the postman.

Oh, how I would have loved to say the *friendly* postman or the *reliable old* postman – but sadly he was neither friendly, terribly reliable or even old for that matter, although age wasn't the important thing. The Important Thing was that he never smiled when a frown would do just as well, and he never whistled for his thin lips were too busy grumbling. He felt that a letter was properly delivered only once it had been dropped in a muddy puddle and ideally stamped upon, and as for parcels ...

Well, on this particular day, (and to be fair to the postman it was a cold, misty sort of a day, when your breath hangs in a damp cloud in front of you and you can't feel your fingers), Pooh could see that he was holding something that *might* once have been a parcel. There was certainly some string hanging from it and, was that brown paper? So hard to tell what with the water dripping from it, making quite a good-sized puddle on the doorstep.

And so, the parcel, if that was what it was, was handed in at the door and what happened to it after that, Pooh didn't see. But I can tell you that it was put beside the hearth in the kitchen to dry out and, in the hustle and bustle of the preparations for Christmas, it was quite forgotten about.

It was only when Pooh saw the lights coming on in the houses on the other side of the street, that he realised just how dark it had become and just how empty his tummy was feeling. Pooh knew that his place was here in the

window and that he shouldn't be seen adventuring unless Christopher Robin was with him, but feeling peckish he made his way downstairs with a

BUMP,

BUMP,

OUCH.

When he reached the foot of the stairs, he heard a muttering and a rustling of paper coming from the kitchen and, peeping round the door, he saw upon the floor the glimpse of a hoof. "A hoof?" I hear you say, yes certainly some kind of a hoof, emerging from the paper. And this is what he heard …

'Eee Orrrrr, Eee Orrrrr. Brown paper indeed and string!

Not that soft, silky a-gift-for-me-ribbon that you see in pinks and blues and greens. Not that merry-Christmas-best-wishes-new-baby-ribbon, but string ... common string, and uncommonly rough string at that ...'

Something or someone emerged from the paper and shook it off, crossly.

But Cook, whose hearing and eyesight weren't as good as Pooh's, saw only a limp grey rag and, as she had spilt some milk, she grabbed the rag and used it to clean up the mess.

Winnie-the-Pooh looked on anxiously. 'A hoof,' he thought to himself, 'generally has some kind of leg attached to it. And a body, a head and so on.' And it suddenly seemed to Pooh that Cook had made a terrible mistake and should be corrected before the owner of the hoof became uncomfortable.

It was then that Pooh spotted something gleaming on the floor under the dresser. And as he leaned further around the door for a proper look, he felt sure he knew what it was. It was the cutter that he had seen Cook use to make his favourite honey biscuits. Cook would roll out the sticky dough and then plunge this very cutter into it to make perfect little circles with fluted edges. Just the thought of it made Pooh's mouth water and his tummy rumble. He thought of the crumbly edges of those biscuits once they were cooked and the trail of sticky honey that criss-crossed over them ... but:

'Eee ... Orrrr. The indignity. The affront. My nose will never be the same again. Eeee ... Orrrrr,' came a muffled voice from the floor, where the poor Hoof-rag was being used very vigorously as a cleaning cloth. There was no time to lose. Pooh *had* to rescue him.

And it was then that Winnie-the-Pooh had an Idea. The sort of Idea that made his nose prickle with pride. Getting down on his tummy and wriggling himself across the floor, he reached and stretched and stretched and reached under the dresser and pulled out the cutter. Then with a push, he sent it rolling across the floor past Cook, past the Hoof-rag and right out of the door into the hallway, where it came to a spinning, clattering stop by the leg of the side table. Straightening up and rubbing her back, Cook went to fetch it, leaving the Hoof-rag in a sorry state on the floor.

Pooh rushed over to where he lay and using all his strength tried to get the Hoof-rag up onto his four wobbly legs. But no sooner was one leg straight than another would buckle and just when all four legs seemed to be working, the creature's far-too-large head lolled forwards and, with the weight of his large ears, he was sent flopping back onto the floor again. Finally, with his head up and legs straight, Pooh led him away to the safety of the dark place behind the door.

'Good afternoon,' ventured Pooh, 'or evening perhaps,' he added, feeling a little shy towards the unfortunate Hoof-rag.

'I see nothing good about it,' the Hoof-rag replied, mournfully. '"Good" might suggest some kind of a welcome. I don't expect a red carpet, as such, or a trumpet fanfare, but … to be squashed in brown paper, dropped in a puddle, stood upon and then used as a common rag …' and here he petered out and began to make loud, heaving sounds that went something like this: 'Eee Orrrrr, Eee Orrrrr.'

The Hoof-rag looked so forlorn and sounded so alarming, that Pooh felt he must step in and be The Welcome. And so, he cleared his throat and began at once and this is how it went:

Though the rain is rather wet

'And what would you know about Wet?' said the Hoof-rag, 'When one can take an ear and squeeze it and make a little river of water, Wet hardly does it justice. Soaked would be a better word. Or Drenched ...'

Pooh ignored this interruption and began again, but more quickly this time:

Though the rain is rather wet
The wind windy, the sky grey (and yet ...)
Today's the day we met
And a warm welcome you will get.

'I, Christopher Robin's Bear,' he announced grandly, with a bow, 'welcome you ...?'

'Nameless,' cut in the sad creature.

'Welcome you, Nameless,' continued Pooh.

'No, no,' Nameless lamented, 'I'm not Nameless. I have no name.'

Pooh, who felt rather put out at having his Welcome interrupted just when he had got going, thought they sounded much the same thing, but trying to remain cheerful said, 'Then I shall name you … Eeyore, because … because of that sound,' and here Pooh hesitated, because he was worried that he had caused offence.

'Eeyore …?' said the Nameless Hoof-rag. 'Eeyore?' he repeated again slightly more loudly and confidently. 'Yes, Eeyore. That has a certain ring to it, I think. Not too formal and yet not too familiar. It's a respectable name and I shall take it.'

And that is how a floppy, grey donkey by the name of Eeyore, came to arrive in Mallord Street, Chelsea, London. It was later discovered that he had been sent as a Christmas gift for Christopher Robin, but what with the rain and the puddle and so on, the label had been mislaid.

Wise people say that the way in which we start out in life has a great deal to do with how we live that life and I can't help wondering if Eeyore's damp and disagreeable arrival, in the hands of the grumpy postman, and his being used as a rag by Cook, contributed to what has been described as a - how shall I put it - not entirely chirpy outlook on life.

But on this particular day, we leave Eeyore somewhat cheered and wandering around his new home, practising his name.

'Eeyore's the name. Allow me to introduce myself: *Eeyore*. What a warm welcome you have shown me, Eeyore, that is.'
And so on.

* * *

Eeyore wasn't the only gift to arrive for the little Christopher Robin. Piglet came That Way, too, although much more quietly. He was simply squeezed through the letterbox one sunny day, as a gift from a neighbour. He was picked up and carried to Christopher Robin, who immediately grasped him tightly in his little fist.

'Hello,' said Pooh, a little uncertainly, when he saw the new, small, pink arrival.

'Heeee!' came the high-pitched reply and then, 'Hiiiiii!' It was all that Piglet could manage, because of the squeezing.

'Quite so,' replied Pooh, politely, as he had no idea what the pink thing had said.

But as Pooh smiled encouragingly at the new arrival there was something about him, perhaps his rather tight green sweater, or perhaps the nervous twitching of his nose that made Pooh sure that they would be the very best of friends.

And Piglet was so pleased to see this bear smiling and agreeing with everything he said that he continued to chat, which sounded something like this:

'Pleeese tii meeeet yiii!'

Later in life, Piglet was inclined to blame his small size on all that squeezing – through the letterbox and by little Christopher Robin – but everyone who ever met Piglet said he was just the perfect size.

* * *

'Is that the end?' asked Christopher Robin. 'Piglet's story is much shorter than Eeyore's.'

'Piglet is *much shorter* than Eeyore,' was the explanation.

Christopher Robin thought about this for a while. It was true, but he wasn't sure what that had to do with the story. He knew that sometimes grown-ups made a story short saying, 'It's very late now. You're tired.' when of course all children know that it's the grown-up who's tired – not them. Still, there it was and both Eeyore and Piglet had arrived, which meant that lots more adventures were just around the corner.

CHAPTER FOUR

*in which Winnie meets another
and Eeyore doesn't*

ND SO THE DAYS TROTTED ALONG, some rainy and some not. And every day was comfortable and friendly and much the same as the day before. But what Pooh didn't notice was that Something was not the same and That Something was Christopher Robin. It's well known that if you stay looking at a thing for a very long time then it hardly changes at all, but if you go away and then come back, catching it by surprise, then it can be very different from when you first looked. This is exactly what happened with Christopher Robin.

At first, Christopher Robin spent a great deal of time looking at the sky or ceiling or whatever it was that happened to be Up, often with his legs and arms flip-flapping in the air, but after some time he seemed to prefer being the other way around with his tummy on the ground and his legs and arms still flap-flipping. But this flapping was different, because sometimes the flaps or flips would move him and Christopher Robin seemed most surprised on finding himself somewhere he hadn't been before. Not long after, Christopher Robin began to want things that he couldn't reach and so one day he gave up on the tummy flip-flap-flopping and pulled himself up tall and after that, except for the occasional flop, there was no stopping him. He was here one moment and then there the next. He could even bump himself up and down the stairs on his bottom. Pooh, who was never very far away, barely noticed these changes, but should an aunt call for tea they would cover their mouth with their hands and exclaim, 'Oh hasn't he grown! One can hardly believe it's the same little boy,' and many other such things. But Christopher Robin would just hide behind the large armchair with his friends around him and take no notice at all.

One very Good Thing about this Growing Up that Christopher Robin had secretly been doing (probably at night when no one was looking) was that he was now big enough to have Interesting Conversations with Pooh. And he was also now big enough to visit the Zoo.

'The what?' said Pooh.

'The Zoo,' said Christopher Robin.

'Oh,' said Pooh, 'is that a kind of surprise?'

'I think so,' replied Christopher Robin, 'with elephants and hippopotamuses in it.'

'Ele-potamuses! And Hippo-phants?' said Pooh, very much excited. He had seen some of these in Christopher Robin's books, but to think they were real …

And the very next day, Christopher Robin, Winnie-the-Pooh, Piglet and Eeyore found themselves at the gates of London Zoo.

It should be explained that Eeyore had been somewhat uncertain about leaving the house … 'Fuss and bother' and 'Trampled by elephants' had been just some of his words about the trip, but here they were.

These were some of the animals that they visited:

THE PENGUINS were playing a funny game of all

pretending to be the same penguin. One would waddle along stiff-shouldered and then all the others would copy him. One would flop beak first into their pool and then all the others would do the same. It seemed to Pooh that it was a game they had been practising for a very long time, as they were exceedingly good at it.

THE LIONS were much more lazy. Piglet was very relieved that they were so far away, snoozing in a patch of sunlight at the far side of their enclosure so that they could hardly be seen at all. They also kept their teeth to themselves, out of sight, which Piglet felt was the Right Thing To Do.

THE GIRAFFES wanted to be seen, and stood very close to the crowd. It quite hurt Pooh's short neck as he put his head right back and looked up, up, up the long neck of the tallest giraffe at its far-away head with blinking eyelashes and slow, leaf-munching mouth. As he gazed at the giraffe, a hum came to him:

To

Be taller

Than a

Tree, I

Wonder

What

You'd

See.

Perhaps the park. Perhaps the town.

Perhaps the train up on the Downs.

And down the Downs, is that the sea?

But	whatever
you	see
whether	land
or sea.	Please
do	tell.
Do	you
see	me?

THE ELEPHANTS, or elepots as Pooh called them absent-mindedly when he was thinking about honey, were picking up hay with their trunks, curling them up and round to carefully place it into their mouths. 'What long trunks!' cried Christopher Robin, as an elephant waded into a pool and showered itself with a

powerful stream of water.

'I thought they had trunks for packing and taking on holiday,' said Piglet, 'but these ones are much more fun!' he added, as a particularly big splash left him standing in a puddle of water.

Christopher Robin laughed and skipped on to see his most favourite animal in the whole zoo, Winnie, who had been rescued and brought to live at London Zoo by a kind Canadian soldier. Winnie the bear was not to be confused with our bear, Winnie-the-Pooh. His name was Winnipeg for long and Winnie for short, but he was not related to Winnie-the-Pooh. This Winnie was much more growly and brown and as big as 3 Winnies (Poohs, not Pegs) standing on each other's heads, which they would never do, but if they did that's how tall they'd be.

The friends were waiting expectantly for the keeper to come and feed the bear a little treat, when suddenly Piglet gasped, 'Where's Eeyore?' And there it was. Eeyore wasn't. That is to say, he wasn't there. Christopher Robin was there because he was holding Pooh's hand

and Piglet was there because he was holding onto Christopher Robin, but nobody was holding Eeyore at all. He was gone.

'I'm sure he was here just a moment ago,' said Christopher Robin and then they all began to talk at once about when they thought they had last seen Eeyore.

Piglet thought Eeyore had said, 'why swim over there

only to swim back again,' about the penguins. But Pooh wasn't so sure. Pooh thought Eeyore has said 'no manners at all!' about the lions. But Christopher Robin didn't think so.

'The lions!' gasped Piglet. 'You don't think they've Got Him, do you?'

At this, Christopher Robin looked rather pale. 'To play with, you mean?' he asked, trying not to cry.

'Oh, certainly to play with,' said Piglet, hurriedly. 'Although we should perhaps go quickly ... just in case they're a little rough,' he added, bravely.

Later, when the story was retold back in the nursery, Pooh explained with great pride, how fast his short, rather stiff legs had moved that day. Really it said a great deal about his affection for Eeyore and very little about his love of Exercise (he had to lie in a corner for two whole weeks to recover). But where were we? Oh yes, the lions ...

It is a Well-Known Fact that lions are Not a Friend of donkeys. Neither are they very friendly, in the wild, towards antelopes, buffaloes or zebras. In fact, the list is very long and would need a good many pencils. But when Christopher Robin and Pooh and Piglet arrived, out of breath, at the lions' enclosure, they were still snoozing as they had been before, and there was no sign of Eeyore at all.

And so, a bigger search began. Piglet chose to look in the parts of the zoo where the smaller animals were. He couldn't quite explain why, but he thought Eeyore was more likely to be near the timid little mice and shrews.

Pooh, who after all the fast moving, was feeling a little eleven o'clockish, thought that Eeyore was most likely to be near the ice-cream shop.

Only Christopher Robin had the good sense to walk back to all the places where they'd already been. He walked backwards to be sure he was doing it right. Backwards past Winnie. Backwards past the elephants. Backwards past the giraffes. Backwards past the lions again, just to be sure. Backwards past the penguins and right back, Backwards that is, to the entrance. And here, or perhaps it was there, at the gate, he found Eeyore.

Eeyore was looking very intently at a big sign with a map of the zoo on it. It was beautifully drawn with

little pictures of all the animals and a big arrow saying "YOU ARE HERE".

'There you are!' said Christopher Robin, very much relieved.

'Perfectly obvious if you ask me,' said Eeyore. 'It even says so here,' he added, nodding at the "YOU ARE HERE".

'So, *this* is the Zoo,' he continued, dreamily. 'A little flat and rather too many Words. But there it is, just as you promised, with all the animals.'

'But Eeyore …' began Christopher Robin, but there he stopped. Eeyore hadn't seen a single Real-Life Animal but, for the first time in a little while, he looked very contented.

'Come on,' smiled Christopher Robin, as he called for Pooh and Piglet to join them. 'It's time to go home.' And so they did.

That night, Pooh couldn't help thinking that perhaps Eeyore was right and the animals were better in pictures, after all. Pictures of them in their wild places where they could be truly wild. Especially Winnipeg the bear.

'One bear in London is probably enough,' thought Pooh to himself, hoping that it could be him.

CHAPTER FIVE

in which a mountain is moved

WHEN POOH BEAR WOKE UP ONE MORNING, he wasn't sure if it *was* the morning. That is to say, it was dark. Terribly, terribly dark.

'Perhaps I'm still dreaming?' said Pooh to himself, and as his dreams were generally full of honey, he licked his lips to see if he could taste any. But this taste was furry ...

'If you don't mind,' came an irritable voice. 'When I want a washing, I'll be sure to ask for it.'

'I'm so sorry,' replied Pooh, without knowing what he was sorry for, or who he was sorry to. 'Where are we?' he continued. 'And who is we?' he added for good measure.

But it was then that the dark above him began to shift and turn. Pooh's nose was pushed down to the place where his toes had been just a moment ago and his feet were pressed into his tummy. It was far more exercise than he had ever done before, and it didn't agree with him, especially on an empty stomach. But as things turned, the lights came on and Pooh found himself on the floor of the nursery with Eeyore, the old grey donkey, grumbling beside him.

'Well of all the indignities. To be licked. I'm not one to Complain but somebody should write a letter ... to somebody else ... about this ...'

'Oh, hallo Eeyore,' said Pooh, cheerfully. 'It's you. And it's me. And there's Piglet over there.'

And there he was. Little Piglet was fast asleep in a corner of the nursery with his trotters over his ears. Pooh was secretly rather proud. It wasn't everyone who could sleep like that. But *his* friend, Piglet, could.

At that moment, there came a noise from above their heads. It was a terrifying, exploding kind of noise. Three explosions in fact. It sounded something like this:

TTISSHHOOOO

TTISSHHOOOO

TTISSHHOOOO

Startled, Piglet woke up with a jump.

'W … w …what was that?' he asked.

'A giant Mooster, I should think,' said Pooh, wisely.

'Or perhaps a Hoozle,' said Eeyore. 'Just my luck to meet a Hoozle today. Of all days,' he added, 'when I'm not feeling up to it.'

Piglet didn't much like the sound of either. 'Perhaps we should go downstairs,' he said, hastily. 'Christopher Robin may be there, and he may Need Us.'

Pooh thought about this for a moment. It was true. He hadn't seen Christopher Robin for several days. Which was unusual. But then again, he hadn't EVER seen a Mooster (or a Hoozle, come to think of it) so he felt that The Right Thing To Do would be to face it and then tell Christopher Robin all about it in a 'it was nothing, just what any bear would do,' kind of a way.

'I, Pooh Bear,' he announced solemnly, 'will find this Moosterhoozle and ask it to hush.' Reluctantly, Piglet agreed to join the adventure, but only because he didn't want to be left on his own.

'You won't be needing me, I suppose,' said Eeyore mournfully.

'Oh, we will,' replied Pooh and his words momentarily brightened Eeyore, until he added, 'we can stand on your back to climb.' And he pointed up at where the noise had come from.

'First the licking and now to be stood upon like a common doormat. But it's what I've come to expect,' muttered Eeyore.

And so, the adventure began. Eeyore planted his legs squarely and braced himself. Pooh clambered up onto his back and with a wibble and a wobble and a 'mind my ears', Piglet scrambled onto Pooh's shoulders and with a heave and a ho and an 'ouch' and a 'mind my eye', Piglet pulled himself up and out of sight. Pooh tried to follow, but wasn't quite tall enough to reach.

'Piglet,' he said seriously, as his paw-tip-stretch turned into a tumble and he landed on his back on the floor. 'There may be a delay with us joining you ...'

TTISSHHOOOO

TTISSHHOOOO

TTISSHHOOOO

'Please come quickly,' squeaked Piglet. 'The sound is coming from behind a mountain.'

'I knew it,' said Eeyore.

'Knew what?' asked Pooh, dusting himself down.

'Knew no good would come of it. Any of it,' Eeyore continued.

But Pooh wasn't listening. An idea was coming to him. An Excellent Idea.

In the nursery there were a good many toys. Christopher Robin was lucky enough to have a number of relatives who would call for tea and pat him on the head, notice how he had grown and then rush off again leaving behind a present for him.

The toy that had caught Pooh's attention was a pile of very fine wooden blocks. Each block had letters, numbers and pictures of interesting animals printed on it. One by one, Pooh dragged the blocks over to where Piglet had climbed up and began to build a staircase. It was rather wobbly and there were some gaps in it, but it was definitely a staircase of sorts and, once it was built, Pooh stood back to admire it and then began the climb. Eeyore followed cautiously behind him, but it wasn't so easy with four legs and sometimes his ears fell over his eyes and sometimes Pooh's bottom got in the way. So, as Pooh finally pulled himself up beside Piglet, a rather unfortunate thing happened …

The D block knocked the F block which bumped into the 4 block and, one by one, down tumbled the staircase and Eeyore with it.

BUMP!

CRASH!

THUD!

'As I said,' said Eeyore, who hadn't. 'Not Structurally Sound.'

But Piglet, the brave Piglet, who had been waiting all this time in the shadow of the mountain, had a plan. Next to him was a cord, and throwing one end down, he shouted, 'Bite on this Eeyore and we'll pull you up.'

'Llltt mmm dwwnnn,' mumbled Eeyore, as Piglet and Pooh used all their strength to haul their friend up ... up ... up ... to ...

TTISSHHOOOO

TTISSHHOOOO

TTISSHHOOOO

went the Moosterhoozle or Hoozlemooster from behind the mountain. The three friends clung together and watched as the mountain began to move. Yes, it certainly moved. First to the left, or was it to the right, and then to the right and then, in the blink of an eye, the mountain was gone and there was Christopher Robin, yawning and rubbing his eyes.

At least they thought it was Christopher Robin, but was it Robstopher Chrispin, for something about him was Not Quite Right.

His eyes were red and his nose was red and his lips were very red but, despite all this there was something very white about him. And when he spoke his voice wobbled.

'Have the lions gone?' he asked. 'There were lions coming out of the writing desk and I flapped my arms as hard as I could and flew up to the ceiling, but my arms were getting tired and the lions were getting closer.'

Pooh and Piglet looked at each other anxiously.

'They've gone,' Pooh said, reassuringly, although he looked at them just to be sure. 'They're back in the writing desk. Look,' he added, pointing at a dark piece of furniture with lions carved into it.

Christopher Robin gathered Pooh, Piglet and Eeyore in his arms. He felt hot, but they didn't complain.

TTISSHHOOOOO

TTISSHHOOOOO

TTISSHHOOOOO

sneezed Christopher Robin. 'Just as I thought,' said Eeyore, who hadn't.

'I have something,' explained Christopher Robin. 'It's called Inflew … Infly … something with flying in it.'

'You already said,' grumbled Eeyore. 'And lions in it, too.'

'But the 'flew' will be gone soon, I think, and then I shan't be so hot,' Christopher Robin explained, wisely.

'Oh, I've got that, too,' sympathised Eeyore, 'only much worse.'

* * *

After that, there was a quiet day with nothing but dry toast and water that tasted all wrong to Christopher Robin. The next day there was toast again, but this time with some melted butter on it and a glass of milk and by the third day, there was hot milk with cocoa and

crumpets, with butter filling the little holes and all dripping with honey. On the honey day, Pooh and Piglet took turns climbing Christopher Robin's knee mountain. Sometimes they slid down like expert skiers and sometimes they waited on the very top for the mountain to suddenly flatten and leave them in a breathless heap amongst the bedclothes.

On the fourth day, Christopher Robin was well enough to walk to the window and look down at the motor cars going past in the London street below. And on the fifth day, everything was back to normal again and Pooh made up this song to celebrate:

When your throat is feeling scratchy,
And your head is very hot.
When your dreams are fierce and snatchy,
And the 'flew' you think you've got.

Gather your friends; make a world in your bed.
Your knees are the mountains, the sun is your head.
The pillow a hill and the sheet a great sea,
With Christopher Robin and Piglet and me.*

*And Eeyore was there, too, but he didn't fit into the rhyme.

CHAPTER SIX

in which we all feel very young

'COME ON, IT'S AN OUTING,' said Christopher Robin, as he grabbed Pooh by the paw, Eeyore by the leg and Piglet by the ear.

'Would Outing involve being Outside?' asked Eeyore, as his ears trailed close to the floor, 'and will the Out be for very long? I don't mean to complain, it's just that I was quite busy being In. In the corner of the nursery to be exact and I was planning to be there till dinner.'

'We'll be back at about quarter past,' replied Christopher Robin, a little vaguely. 'But what were you doing in the corner?'

Very pleased to have been asked, Eeyore replied, 'I was contemplating whether large rooms have larger corners than small rooms.'

'Oh, I see,' said Christopher Robin, not quite sure that he did. 'Well, where we are going is sure to have lots of big rooms and corners.'

'Will we be back in time for lunch?' asked Pooh, who always liked to be sure when the next meal would be.

'Don't worry,' smiled Christopher Robin. 'We've got a picnic.'

'"Picnic" is an excellent word,' thought Pooh. 'It has sunshine in it and food, of course, and it sounds skippy and jumpy.'

And so they set off to wherever it was they were going. It was an Explaining kind of a day, with a clear sky and a gentle breeze that lifted words like, "so you see, Pooh," and "that's how it is" up the knobbly tree trunks with bark that you could pull away with your fingers like stiff, curled paper. There were other words that Christopher Robin said too, like "museum" and "fossil", but much as Pooh tried to listen, that Picnic seemed to be calling to him.

Christopher Robin was just about to tell him about dinosaurs, when Pooh asked as politely as he could manage, 'Is it perhaps time for a little taster, a little smackerel of something to help with all the walking?'

'Silly old bear,' laughed Christopher Robin, kindly. 'We haven't even got to the museum yet and there's so much to see before lunchtime.'

'Quite,' said Pooh, 'but I hope there will be a lunchtime. I should hate for it to feel forgotten about.' But it was at that moment that they arrived in front of the museum. 'It's honey-coloured!' Pooh observed, hungrily.

Piglet spotted a large-beaked and winged gargoyle looking down at them. 'What's that?' he thought, alarmed, hoping they wouldn't get too close to it.

For this museum was a very special place. There were hundreds of stone animals and plants hiding all around it. Some of the pillars seemed to be made of twining vines and in other places, cheeky monkeys peeped out of nooks and crannies.

Once inside, Christopher Robin left the picnic with Pooh while he went off with the others to decide where to visit first. 'I'll just check to make sure it's all there,' thought Pooh. And it was. There was one big sandwich for Christopher Robin wrapped up in a blue checked cloth and another for Pooh and Piglet to share, wrapped up in red. There was nothing for Eeyore because he'd said, 'picnics don't agree with me' and 'all those crumbs and nowhere to wash'.

Pooh pushed his nose into the red package. It smelled delicious. 'Perhaps a little nibble now,'

he thought, 'just to sustain me.'

'Is it lunchtime?' asked a small voice a little while later, as Piglet's hungry eyes gazed up at Pooh, expectantly. Pooh looked down at the checked cloth. There was nothing in it apart from several crumbs. One was biggish for a crumb, but terribly small for a lunch. 'Ah,' began Pooh ... 'that is to say...' he continued, wondering what he would

say, but then something caught his attention. High above Piglet's head was a tree. This was odd because they were indoors, but there was certainly a branch at least and the leaves on that branch were those sort of rounded inny outy ones that meant one thing ... acorns! And as you may or may not know, acorns were Piglet's most favourite food in the world.

'I'll be right back,' announced Pooh. And he set off. As luck would have it, there was some kind of knobbly ladder leading up to the branch. It wasn't a normal ladder as such, but it had ridges that did very well for

steps for an Intrepid and Brave Bear. Up, and Up Pooh went. If I were to write an 'Up' for every Up that Pooh upped then I'd pretty soon run out of paper, but on and on he climbed.

'I'm coming,' called Pooh down to Piglet, who was very far below by now.

'It looks to me like you're still going,' called up Piglet. 'You're getting higher and smaller, which generally means Going not Coming.'

Pooh didn't feel smaller as he huffed and puffed his way along the ladder. In fact, he rather wished that he was, because he had to carry his full-of-lunch tummy with him. But remembering his lunch reminded him about Piglet's, which made him all the more determined to reach those acorns.

'Soon,' called Pooh.

'Do be careful,' Piglet replied hopefully and distantly from below.

'Oh, I'm quite all right,'

called Pooh, confidently. 'Bears are very good at finding lunches and ...' but we'll never know what else bears were very good at because it was at that moment that Pooh reached the end of the ladder. And the end had TEETH!

The Intrepid Bear made a wild grab at an acorn hanging above him and raced back the way he'd come at great speed, falling with a

LUMPITY,

BUMPITY,

BUMP,

down the knobbly ladder much faster than he had gone up it.

'That was quick!' said Piglet, alarmed, as he saw poor Pooh coming back down in what can only be described as a very hiccup-y way.

'Here's your lunch,' said Pooh, a little breathlessly,

as he rubbed his bruised bottom. 'I would have brought more only something with teeth seemed to have got there before me.'

Piglet took the acorn from Pooh. 'Thank you,' he said, deciding it was best not to mention that it was made of some kind of shiny rubber and not meant to be eaten. He quietly left it at the base of the imitation tree.

'Isn't the Diplodocus glorious,' said Christopher Robin, joining them whilst munching on his sandwich.

'The Dippywhat-cus?' asked Pooh. 'Is she the one with teeth?'

'Docus - Diplodocus,' explained Christopher Robin. 'Yes, lots of teeth but only for eating plants - she's a herbivore.'

Piglet thought that they must be very good teeth if they could manage the rubber acorns, but he didn't say anything.

After that they saw many more dinosaurs. They saw a Triceratops with three pointy horns. Eeyore thought it should have been called the Threehornsontops.

'They all have such long names,' remarked Piglet. 'It must have taken them a long time to learn to write them down.' And Christopher Robin, who was just discovering this problem because he was learning to write his own rather-too-long name, agreed that short names like "It" were much better for writing.

They also saw a Stegosaurus, which had bony plates all along its back. He was Pooh's favourite. He was huge, but they were told his brain was no bigger than a plum. 'It's wonderful how big you can grow with hardly any brain at all,' marvelled the Bear of Very Little Brain, looking down at his own impressive tummy.

'These dinosaurs were alive 65 million years ago,' explained Christopher Robin. 'That's 6 noughts,' he added proudly.

'Is that before last Wednesday?' asked Pooh. 'Before the time Eeyore fell asleep with his nose in the jelly?'

'I fail to see,' said Eeyore, blushing a little, 'why that Unfortunate Incident is in any way relevant.'

'Long, long before that,' said Christopher Robin. 'Before I was born and perhaps even before Grandmother was born, but probably not. In any case, hundreds and hundreds of lunches and teas ago.'

This mention of lunch reminded Pooh that whilst he had had one, and Piglet's too of course, he could probably manage a little lick of honey and he knew there was some waiting for him at home.

'I think,' said Pooh to no one in particular, 'that the Dippy-docus and the Threehornisaurus and the …' and here he paused because although long words were

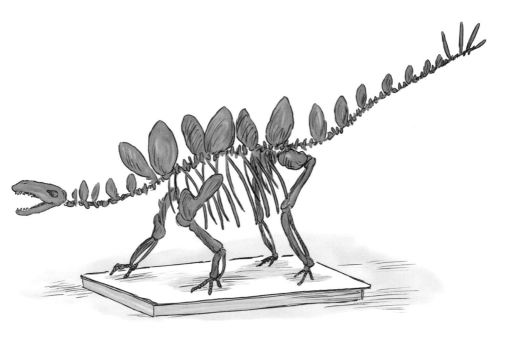

bothersome for him, he wanted to get this one right, '… the Steg-OH-saw-us and all the other dinosaurs might be tired what with being so very, very old, so perhaps we had better leave them to sleep and go home for a little smackerel of something.'

The others were quick to agree. Eeyore in particular seemed very anxious to get back to his corner of the nursery to see how it compared with the corners in the museum. As they made their way home, Pooh kept everyone cheerful with a special-SAURUS hum, which started as a whisper and got louder and louder:

[whisper]
  Stego-SAURUS
  Stego-SAURUS
    Tiptoe, tiptoe …
      He's ignored us!

    [louder]
      Marsho-SAURUS
      Marsho-SAURUS
      Quickly, quickly
      Before she claws us!

      [really, really loud]
      Allo-SAURUS
      Allo-SAURUS
      Run away
      Or else she'll gnaw us!

And, for the rest of the walk home, even Eeyore joined in pretending to run away from the terrible sandwich-stealing Picnic-a-saurus, otherwise known as Winnie-the-Pooh!

CHAPTER SEVEN

in which it rains, a great deal

'PAH! RAINING AGAIN. I KNEW IT,' Eeyore would complain happily to himself. He loved the plink, plonk, splish, splosh sound it made on the roof.

'I can hardly hear myself think!' he'd exclaim.

He loved the way that everything outside the rain-splashed nursery window looked soft, blurred and gloomy, but most of all he loved racing raindrops down the windowpane. Well, he didn't actually race them, of course. He sat completely still and watched them fall. He even liked it when the raindrop he had chosen to win, didn't.

'Typical. You choose the biggest, wobbliest drop,' he would say to anyone who would listen. 'It's ready to tumble down the window and then some little drip comes out of nowhere and befriends two or three other little drips and together they join up and win. Pah!'

This game would keep him happily occupied staring at the window for many hours, while behind him another game was being played. Christopher Robin, Pooh and

Piglet were building a den. It was to be the biggest, best den they had *ever* built.

'With rooms,' said Piglet.

'Oh, yes, lots and lots of rooms,' agreed Pooh, as he pulled all the covers down from Christopher Robin's bed. 'And a larder.'

'A larder?' came Piglet's muffled voice from underneath the covers. 'What's that?'

'It's where you keep things,' explained Pooh, crawling out from the pile of sheets and blankets.

'Like interesting stones?' asked Piglet.

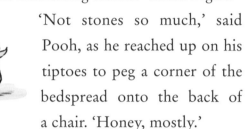

'Not stones so much,' said Pooh, as he reached up on his tiptoes to peg a corner of the bedspread onto the back of a chair. 'Honey, mostly.'

Christopher Robin wasn't sure that honey and bedclothes were such a good combination, but he didn't say anything.

Now, building a den is not as easy as it might sound. There's the problem of the roof, and the problem of the walls. Sometimes the roof forgets to stay up and sometimes

the walls are all window and no wall at all. Piglet made several very good rooms that Christopher Robin couldn't fit inside and Pooh accidentally trod on one of them while Piglet was in it, which was unfortunate and slightly painful. But little by little, the den started to look a bit more den-ish or some would say "den-like". Either way, it began to resemble one.

'Where's the other peg?' asked Pooh. 'The one that was by my foot.'

Piglet didn't know.

'And where's my green jumper?' asked Piglet.

'If you mean your sweater,' said Christopher Robin, 'you're wearing it.'

But Piglet explained, at great length, how it was a jumper not a sweater and that there wasn't just One. There was the green one he was wearing, the green one he had just worn yesterday and the green one he was going to wear tomorrow. 'Tomorrow's jumper has gone,' he said, decidedly.

'Tomorrow will always be gone in two days' time,' came a mournful voice from up by the window.

The den builders ignored this interruption.

'Have you ever noticed,' said Christopher Robin, 'how a great many things go missing, like all the red crayons and the best rubber that actually rubs things out? And now the peg and Piglet's sweater. It's Most Mysterious and we should Investigate.'

Eeyore suggested that they leave some tempting objects just outside the den. 'Then you three hide quietly and leave me in peace … I mean,' he quickly corrected himself, 'watch to see what happens.'

And so they placed a dice and a little box in front of the den and crept inside.

'It's called Oddserving,' explained Christopher Robin, helpfully, and Piglet and Pooh nodded, pretending they knew what he was talking about.

And so there, in their best-ever den, they waited for what felt like days and days, but was really just the time it took for the big hand on the clock on the mantlepiece to move from pointing straight up at the ceiling to pointing

at the dappled rocking horse, as if to say that it was time to gallop around the nursery. And while they waited for Something To Happen, Pooh hummed a little hum to pass the time:

> A Bear and a Piglet built a great den
> With a ho and a hum and a diddly-um
> There they lay waiting and then ...
> With a ho and a hum and a diddly-um
> They waited some more and then some more ...
> With a ho and a hum and a diddly-um
> Until the Piglet began to snore.
> With a ...

'I didn't!' said Piglet, indignantly. It was true that his eyes had begun to feel a little heavy and fluttery in the cosy den, but he certainly hadn't snored!

'At least you were in the hum,' said Christopher Robin, a little put out. But it was at just that moment that *Something* moved in the corner of the nursery. Then Something scurried across the floor. Something was now sniffing around the tempting objects.

'Ho!' called out Pooh Bear, bravely.

'Hum!' joined in Piglet, from the safe place of directly

behind Pooh. And Christopher Robin was just about to get to the most terrifying part, the 'Diddly-um', when Pooh tripped over a skittle, which bumped the chair, which toppled the broom handle, which twanged the string, which pulled down the woolly blanket, which made everything terribly, terribly dark.

'Something has trapped us!' squealed the little Piglet.

'Quickly!' called out Christopher Robin, 'or Something will get away with the tempting objects!' But the tricky thing is knowing which direction to go quickly in, when you have wool in your eyes and fluff in your mouth.

'This looks fun!' came a small, confident voice from the other side of the blanket. 'Can I play, too?'

'We're not playing,' said Pooh, a little sharply. 'We're Oddserving and Investigating and … and …'

'… trying to get out,' finished, Piglet, helpfully.

On hearing this, the Something ran, better than any acrobat, along the length of the broom. She wasn't very heavy, but her weight was just enough to … tip … tip … tip the broom, which lifted up a corner of the blanket, making a small doorway for Christopher Robin, Pooh and Piglet to crawl out of.

'Thank you,' said Piglet, looking at the stranger and quickly pulling himself up to his full height. He had never had the pleasure of meeting someone smaller than himself before, and he rather liked it. Then he remembered his green jumper.

'Have *you* been taking our things?' Piglet asked, rather boldly, and then he blushed at his own boldness and pretended to be very busy with something behind him instead.

'Oh, no,' said the small mouse, who told them her name was Flo. 'I take things people don't want any more, and I make them into something even better. Come and look!' And with that she scampered away to the corner of the nursery, and it was all the others could do to keep up with her.

'Look in there,' said Flo, proudly.

At first the friends weren't sure exactly where they were meant to be looking, but then Piglet noticed the hole at the bottom of the skirting board. Lying side by side, flat on their stomachs, the friends looked through it. This wasn't so easy with Pooh's honey-filled stomach, but with a bit of wriggling they all managed to get a peep into the most magical place they had ever seen.

'Oooh!' gasped Christopher Robin and Pooh, both in a state of great wonderment, as they gazed at the miniature swings and stairs and slides. Everything was made out of the most Ordinary things, the sort of bits and bobs you trip over and grumble about when your toes are stubbed. But put together by nimble mousey paws, they were quite Extraordinary.

'Oh my!' added Piglet, as he took in the tiny, marvellous mouse playground. At the centre of it all there was the most splendid little trampoline. Flo bounced up and down on it and turned somersaults to show them how it worked. It was a beautiful green colour … a very familiar green colour.

'It's your sweater!' said Pooh in surprise.

'No, it's my jumper,' replied Piglet, 'and just look how good at jumping it is!'

Flo looked at them, quizzically.

'I think you may have mistakenly taken tomorrow's jumper,' explained Piglet, 'but really yesterday's jumper will do very well for tomorrow.' And he sighed a happy sigh to think that he had somehow been a part of making this magic happen.

'I love to invent, create and build,' said Flo, as she bounced right off the trampoline and came hurtling down a slide that led to a spoon, coming to a stop right by the hole. 'I've made so many things that I can't count them all. But I build the best things on rainy days.'

'Rainy days are a Good Thing,' said Christopher Robin, admiringly. 'Of course, Pooh, Piglet and I also invented a … umm, that is to say created a … or rather built a splendid … ummm … thing,' he continued, not quite sure what to call their collapsed den.

'But we had a bit of botheration with the broom and so on,' added Pooh.

'Pah!' came a sound from up above them by the window. 'You call that building? I call it hours of tidying up afterwards.' And Eeyore was so pleased with his observation, that he missed seeing which of his raindrops got to the bottom of the window first.

'Don't mind Eeyore,' continued Christopher Robin. 'He's not so much of a Builder. He's more of an Adviser. Perhaps next time you could help us, Flo?'

Flo nodded, enthusiastically.

* * *

'And did the little mouse, Flo, help?' asked Christopher Robin. 'I think she did, but I can't remember. She seemed a lot better at building than us,' he added, yawning. 'I love rain. I hope it rains every day, forever,' he added, as he listened to the gentle pitter-patter on the roof.

CHAPTER EIGHT

*in which some hiding places are
better than others*

'**D**ON'T YOU REMEMBER LONDON AT ALL?' asked
Christopher Robin, somewhat surprised. 'We've
only been away for two days.'

'London ...' said Pooh dreamily, 'was that the place
before we lived in trees? The place where you went
through iron gates to get to the Forest?'

'Perhaps you're thinking of the park,' said Christopher
Robin. 'It's like the Forest, only smaller and the flowers
grow in rows.'

'I remember the rows of noisy red monsters,' shuddered
Piglet. 'Those spluttering, coughing beasts who gobbled
up people and rode away with them inside.'

'I think those were buses,' said Christopher Robin, but
he couldn't be sure because he was beginning to forget
about London himself. The Forest had made Christopher
Robin forget. Its breezes had blown the city dust off his
clothes. Its birdsong had chased the city noises out of his
ears. Its streams had tempted his city shoes off his feet
and Christopher Robin had paddled for hours, until the

shoes were quite forgotten. Other things were forgotten too, like what two times two o'clock was and how many 'I's were in 'goodbye'.

'It's about time!' said an important-looking rabbit, who had marched up to where Christopher Robin, Pooh and Piglet lay on a grassy slope.

'Time for a little snack?' asked Pooh, hopefully.

'Time you Arrived,' replied the rabbit, a little sharply. 'We've been Waiting.'

'Oh,' said Pooh, sitting up a little straighter and trying to look like he'd been worth waiting for. 'Thank you. I mean to say … sorry.'

'Yes, well it can't be helped, I suppose,' said the rabbit, briskly. 'Still there it is. I've so much to do. I must tell Owl all about it.' And with that, he hurried away.

'Do you know him?' asked Piglet. 'He seemed to know us. Or was waiting for us or something …' he tailed off uncertainly.

'That's just Rabbit,' said Christopher Robin. 'He's always terribly busy trying not to be late for things. But if you're always early, then people might think you're late for the thing before. That's the sort of thing that worries Rabbit.'

'Oh,' said Pooh, who had found it very hard to be worried about anything since he'd arrived in the Forest. Of course, there was always that little worry about a cloudy day turning stormy. But really, storm clouds only meant that it was time to go home and find a little something to nibble on, so sometimes Pooh felt more inclined to worry that the clouds weren't as stormy as he hoped they might be.

'I see that you've Started Without Me,' said a familiar voice. 'As Usual,' he added.

'I don't think we've Started,' said Pooh. 'Rabbit said we'd Arrived At Last. But I don't think I was last. Perhaps you were Eeyore?'

'The cheek of it,' said Eeyore, more than a little put out. 'To call me Last. Last indeed and then to Start Without Me.'

'Start what, Eeyore?' asked Piglet, who hated to disappoint his good friend.

'The game, of course,' Eeyore continued. 'I'm not surprised, though. After all, who would want a donkey to play with? A donkey is no good for games.'

Christopher Robin was pretty sure that they weren't playing a game, although now that he thought of it, that did sound like a good plan.

'Of course you're good for games, Eeyore,' he said, kindly. 'I'll tell Rabbit, his friend Owl and all the others that we're playing and then you, Eeyore, will hide and we'll all close our eyes and count, and then come looking for you.'

'Are we playing hide-and-seek?' asked Piglet excitedly. 'I'm good at that!' And then he started to tell them about the time when he had hidden in the nursery and no one had found him for a whole week.

'That was because you were the only one playing,' remarked Eeyore. 'You were lucky it wasn't longer than a week.'

'Yes, that's the game,' said Christopher Robin. 'But this time we're going to try it a different way. The hider hides and the first finder hides with them and then the second finder hides with the first finder and the hider and so on. Do you see?'

They didn't see, but they decided to try it anyway. Pooh always found that when anyone explained the rules of a game to him, the words danced around his head and tickled his ears and sat on his eyelids until they were so heavy that they closed. Really, the only way to know a game was to play it and so, now that everyone was gathered, they began with Eeyore hiding and everyone else counting.

Now, as you may know, counting out loud with your eyes closed, with others who put the numbers a different way around to you, is a very muddling thing to do. Piglet liked the numbers one, two and three the best and so he said them over and over again. Whereas Owl preferred long numbers like five hundred, two thousand and forty-six, so he counted using those numbers and no one really seemed to know what number they were stopping at. After a few moments, Christopher Robin said, 'Coming ready or not!' and they were all happy to leave the numbers behind and set off to search for Eeyore.

As Pooh searched, he made up a hum:

I'm looking for ...
Looking for ...
Looking for ... Who?
Looking for Pooh?
No, Pooh's the one looking. Pooh's the one seeking.
Pooh did the counting without ever peeking.
So, join in the hunt, join in with Pooh.
Just whatever you do, don't ask, 'For who?'

'Whom,' said a voice. It was Owl.

'It can't be "whom",' explained Pooh, 'because of the "Poohmm".'

'Well it isn't a very good poohmm, poem that is,' continued Owl, severely, 'if no one is paying attention to the dative case.'

But while Pooh was having a problem remembering who or whom he was looking for, Christopher Robin was having a completely different problem ... And the Problem was Eeyore. He *had* found Eeyore. 'Very good' I hear you say, but the problem was *where* he'd found him. He'd found Eeyore standing in the middle of a shallow stream. If you were being kind you could have said that his feet were a little bit hidden, perhaps even his lower legs, but certainly no more than that. If you were being less kind you might say that of all the places in the Forest to hide it was the Very Worst – especially if the finders were expected to hide there, too.

'Well Eeyore,' said Christopher Robin, 'that's a very good place to hide ... if you're a pebble ... or a fish.'

'I told you that donkeys were no good at games. But would you listen?' lamented Eeyore.

'Never mind,' said Christopher Robin. 'Let's hide in that large hole over there.' And so, they did.

They squeezed and they squashed and then BUMP, they landed in their hiding place, making so much noise that Pooh heard and peered into the hole.

'You have to hide here too now,' explained Christopher Robin. But whilst the hole was certainly a better hiding place than the stream, it wasn't very big. It led to a smallish burrow and, what with Pooh's generous tummy, and all the bits of furniture, it was becoming rather cramped.

Then Owl pressed his large wings close to his sides and squeezed in as well.

'I would advise,' he counselled, wisely, 'that the diaphragm in the pulmonary region be contracted through an inhalation.'

'He says we should all breathe in,' explained Christopher Robin.

'That's all very well,' complained Eeyore. 'But ...'

'Found you!' squeaked a small voice. Luckily, the voice belonged to little Piglet, who squeezed himself in behind Eeyore.

'That's all very well,' complained Eeyore, more loudly, 'But ...'

'Found you! Found you! Found you!' came a chorus of Rabbit-related voices, one of them Rabbit's own and others from various friends and relations, some of whom had come in a different door altogether probably because it was their kitchen that was being hidden in.

After that, it became very hard to tell which way was up, which foot belonged to who, and a stool that had started off as something to sit on became a kind of hat. But there the friends stayed ... and stayed ... and stayed. Until Eeyore found enough breath to say: 'It's all very well, BUT when does the game finish?'

'It finishes when we're all here,' explained Christopher Robin.

'Hmm,' said Eeyore. 'And does anyone happen to know how many All is?'

At this everyone went quiet. But then Pooh had an idea. Perhaps his best idea since he arrived in the Forest.

'Piglet will count to three,' he said. 'And then everyone who's here should say "Here" and then we'll know we're all Here and we can then go somewhere else.'

And so, as Piglet finished his best ever counting in his loudest counting voice, there was a chorus of 'Here! Here!'

It's best not to describe how everybody got out of that burrow. It certainly wasn't very dignified. Several tails were trodden upon, bottoms were bumped and one friend or relation sat in a pie.

That evening, as Pooh and Piglet walked back to their houses, they talked about all the new friends they had met in the Forest.

'I wasn't sure about Owl, at first,' admitted Piglet. 'His beak looked sharp, but he was very good at counting.'

Pooh agreed. 'That game was rather uncomfortable, but now that I've played it, I do feel that we've Arrived. Just as Rabbit said we had. And that's a very good thing.'

And with that, they wished each other goodnight and disappeared through the little doors to their homes inside the trees.

CHAPTER NINE

in which several holes are dug

A DEEP VOICE WOKE WINNIE-THE-POOH FROM his comfortable armchair nap. Then there was a swooshing noise right outside his front door, followed by the sound of broken branches a little further off.

'I must invest ... in-nest ... nest-in a-gate ... vest-in-a gate. Oh bother, that's not right,' Pooh sighed to himself. 'I must go and find out what's happening,' he finished quickly. Sometimes words came to Pooh and sometimes they didn't. Today they didn't so very much, but there it was and the Important Thing, he thought to himself, was that he should find out what was making those sounds and then tell Christopher Robin all about it.

And so, rather cautiously, he followed the strange noises. The deep voice seemed to be saying 'Arrrr' in quite a menacing way and the swooshing was getting louder now and 'Ohh!' gasped Pooh, as the swoosh swooshed right past his nose.

'Ahoy there, Bear!' said the deep voice. 'I'm taking you captive.'

Perhaps Pooh should have been frightened but although the face glaring down at him had an eye covered with a black patch the other eye looked very much like …

'Christopher Robin?' said Pooh. 'Is that you?'

'No,' said Christopher Robin, 'It's Captain Billy the Terrible. All the Forest fears me and my mighty cutlass,' he continued, waving around the thing that had swooshed and which looked to Pooh very much like a stick.

'Oh,' said Pooh. 'I thought it was Christopher Robin, but perhaps it wasn't.' And he sat down on the grass to think about it.

All the 'Arrs' and swooshing had drawn the other animals out from their homes. Soon there was quite a crowd gathered around Pooh and Billy the Terrible.

'What's going on here?' enquired Rabbit, importantly, for he always liked to be The First To Know.

'This is Christopher-Billy, I mean, Robin, that is to say, Captain Billy the Terrible,' said Pooh. 'And I'm Captive and am being taken somewhere … I think,' he continued, looking a bit confused.

'We're playing at pirates,' explained the pirate. 'I've been reading about them in my book with the big pictures. We need to bury some treasure,' he continued, taking off his splendid eye patch.

'Oh, it is you, Christopher Robin,' sighed little Piglet, who had been listening, nervously, all this time. 'I thought it was. Then you said it wasn't.'

'Perfectly obvious, if you ask me,' said Eeyore, 'although, as usual, nobody did. However I mustn't complain, just the other week I was asked the time. As if I care to know about the time when it goes so slowly in my gloomy place,' he continued.

'Well, anyway,' said Christopher Robin. 'We must all hide some treasure and perhaps in a million years someone will come along and find it and it will tell them lots about the olden days.'

The animals were very much impressed. It seemed like a Grand Idea to have secret treasure hidden all around the Forest just waiting a million or so years to be found.

'What should the treasure be?' asked Piglet, breathless with excitement and ready to begin.

'Well,' said Christopher Robin, thoughtfully, 'pirates normally bury jewels and golden coins but I'm not sure where to get those, so I thought I'd bury these.'

And, with that, he turned out his pockets and this is what fell onto the grass:

One toy soldier (whose little stand had broken off so he could only lie down and wasn't much good to play with.)

One little spinning top (painted with bright colours which, when the top spun, all blurred together.)

And one large glass marble (which caught the light beautifully and, if you looked carefully, you could see bright blue swirls inside, which reminded Christopher Robin of the sea and so seemed just the right thing for a pirate's treasure.)

'For my treasure,' announced Eeyore grandly, 'I shall bury this stone.' And here he pointed at what looked to the others like a fairly normal-ish stone, the sort of stone you wouldn't even bother to trip over. 'This stone,' continued Eeyore, 'marks the place where I once found a particularly fine thistle to eat. I marked it with a stone for later and, when I returned, there was the stone but NO THISTLE.'

'But Eeyore,' suggested Pooh, helpfully. 'Are you sure it was *this* stone? There's another one very much like it there,' he said, pointing a little to the right, 'and another there … Perhaps the thistle is near to a different stone?'

'Are you suggesting?' boomed Eeyore, in a very grave voice. 'That I don't know my own stone? A stone placed by me, Eeyore?'

Pooh realised that this was exactly what he was suggesting but he was in a great hurry to get started with his own treasure, so he mumbled an apology to Eeyore, who at once began to dig a hole with his hoof. The difficulty was that the ground Eeyore had chosen for burying his treasure was particularly stony and so he had to kick away a good many stones to make space for *his* stone but, at last, it was buried.

And then the others set to work.

Piglet buried some special pieces of pottery and coloured glass that he had found not so long ago. He kept the best one with the blue and white pattern on it, but he buried the others in the Sandy Place, where it was ever so much easier to dig than where Eeyore's treasure was buried. Rabbit hurried home and found one of his longest and most impressive lists. It had things on it like: AT ONCE and IMPORTONT. He rolled it up and buried it under a hedge, very pleased by how impressed those people in a million years would be when they saw quite how busy the owner of the list had been.

Some of Rabbit's friends and relations seemed to have misunderstood the task and the middle-sized relations were trying to bury the smaller ones. But after a great deal of noise and fuss, they went away to bury some small objects that weren't relations.

Owl, who at first had felt himself a little too Grand and Wise to play at pirates, was, on reflection, very much taken with the idea of Communicatering With Future Generations, as he put it. In fact, he got a little carried away, and buried a great many things that he later wished he hadn't, including his slippers.

Pooh seemed to be the only one in the Forest who didn't have treasure to bury. He walked around for some time, trying to think of something and to help with his thoughts he made up a hum:

> A pirate sailed the seven seas
> With an 'Arr' and a 'Grrr' and a swoosh of his sword.
> But however hard that pirate tried
> He couldn't find a treasure hoard.
>
> And however hard he swooshed his sword
> He couldn't find a treasure hoard.

As he went along, he put a great deal of effort into the 'Arrs' and the 'Grrrs' and he waved his stick with such dramatic swooshes that he didn't even notice that he had 'Arr'd' and 'Grr'd' and swooshed all the way back to his own front door.

'Well, here I am,' said Winnie-the-Pooh, a little surprised. And with that he went inside and wasn't seen by anyone for some time.

* * *

When the friends did all meet again, Christopher Robin had gathered long branches and had built a wonderful den that stood up by leaning on itself. Everyone squeezed inside to listen to pirate stories. After the part where

Billy the Terrible had jumped overboard, fought a giant shark and swum, or was it swam, with all his might to the shore, Pooh began to feel a little peckish. He was sure it was about the time of day when a little smackerel was called for. Without disturbing the others, he crawled out of the den and went to a place under the trees where two sticks lay in a cross. Carefully, he moved the sticks to one side and started to dig. He dug, and he dug, until he began to feel that he should give up, but then he heard a sound. It was a pot-ish sound. And with a ginormous heave, he pulled up a pot of honey that was almost as big as himself and very carefully, he carried it back to the den.

Christopher Robin was very much surprised to see a large pot wobbling towards him and only a little less surprised when he saw Pooh carrying it.

'Where did you find that?' he asked.

'Oh, just over there,' said Pooh, casually. 'I dug a little and there it was, just there in the ground. But treasure is like that, I suppose, sometimes it's there and sometimes it isn't.'

'Pooh Bear,' said Christopher Robin solemnly, 'you are the very first of us pirates to find real, actual Treasure. This means that you are now the Chief Pirate,' and with a flourish, he handed Pooh the eye patch and Piglet helped him put it over his left eye. Pooh blinked behind the eye patch, proudly.

Christopher Robin continued with his story and at the end he said, 'You never did tell us, Pooh, what the treasure was that you had buried to be found in a million years.'

But, in the warmth of the den, Chief Pirate Pooh Bear was already fast asleep with his back against the empty honey jar and his chin resting on his full stomach.

CHAPTER TEN

in which we all live happily ever after. The end.

'**M**OVE ALONG THERE. QUICKLY PLEASE,' instructed Rabbit, as an assortment of animals formed a disorderly line in front him.

Rabbit had been in this 'line-up, listen-please, hurry-along' kind of a mood ever since he had woken up to see a hard frost covering the whole of the Forest like a sprinkling of crisp, white, shivery sugar. And the reason for all this lining up was that Rabbit had Important Information to share.

'Does Important Information need us to be in a line?' pondered Pooh out-loud, to himself.

'Important Information,' explained Rabbit, 'needs to be heard. And hearing means ears facing forward.' At this, Eeyore flapped his ears. 'Mine face down, mostly,' he lamented, drooping his head towards the hard, cold ground.

'I've gathered you all here,' announced Rabbit firmly, 'because of a Danger.'

'A stranger, did you say?' asked Eeyore. 'Only I

couldn't quite hear on account of my downwards ears and that cracking sound.'

'A Danger, not a stranger,' replied Rabbit, who was interrupted by Christopher Robin coming towards them. He was always a very cheering person to see, but today something was Different. And the Difference was the tallest, bluest, shiniest pair of wellington boots that were ever seen.

'Oh my,' gulped Piglet, who had never seen a bluer blue.

'Splendid,' confirmed Rabbit, who appreciated a clean pair of boots no matter what the colour.

'Impermeable,' commended Owl.

But Eeyore was agitated. 'There is a sound coming from the ground,' he said.

'What did you say, Eeyore?' asked Christopher Robin, coming closer.

'I was saying …' announced Eeyore, but he immediately stopped saying what he was saying, for at that moment everyone heard it.

Tink! Tink! CRACK!

And the ground underneath them began to shift and split showing that it wasn't ground at all, but ice. And the ice was cracking!

With a slip and a slide and an 'ouch that's my tail!' and a 'just give me a push, will you?' the animals scrambled off the ice, but Christopher Robin couldn't. Christopher Robin was stuck. That is to say, his left boot was stuck.

'As I was saying,' continued Rabbit, 'with this cold weather there is a Danger of Ice.'

'Pah,' grumbled Eeyore. 'Ice! And where does he gather us to talk about this ice? On the ice! Perfect! A practical demonstration.' And he was just beginning to feel very pleased with his observations, when he remembered that Christopher Robin was still on, or perhaps more accurately stuck in, the ice.

'Could I bump you out,' asked Pooh, bravely stepping forward to help.

'Not wise,' explained Rabbit, pointing at the Danger.

'I can do it by myself,' said Christopher Robin and with a tug … and a heave … and a POP he was out of the ice. But his boot wasn't. 'They were the very best boots I ever had,' said Christopher Robin, as he stood on one leg looking at the lone, beautiful boot wedged in the ice.

'One is something to be thankful for,' observed Eeyore, but Christopher Robin wasn't sure

how useful one boot would be and, a little down-hearted, but with great style, he Hop, Hop, Hopped all the way home on his one remaining blue boot.

'A watch must be formed,' announced Rabbit to the animals who had stayed to gaze at the boot.

'I have a clock at my house,' said Pooh.

'Watch, as in To Look,' returned Rabbit.

'I'll look for it right away,' said Pooh, more determined than ever to be helpful.

'By a Watch,' said Rabbit, a little crossly, 'I mean a Lookout. A guard to Watch the boot to make sure that nothing happens to it.' And so, it was agreed that the animals would take turns watching the boot.

Pooh and Piglet offered to go first. Pooh had never been a Watch before and hoped that Piglet would know what to do and Piglet, who had noticed heavy grey clouds forming above them in this particularly lonely part of the Forest, thought two Watchers were sure to be better than one. And so, the others wandered away to their warm trees and burrows, leaving Pooh and Piglet huddled together on the tufty, frosty grass.

After a while of saying nothing much, Pooh said: 'All this boot business is making me remember that I missed my lunch last Wednesday and so I should probably go home and find it before somebody else does.'

Piglet said he would be just fine by himself for a little while, but no sooner had Pooh gone than a cold wind blew, and large, wet flakes of snow began to fall.

'I-i-i-it's t-t-t-terribly c-c-c-cold, all of a sudden,' Piglet said, his teeth chattering so loudly that he had to shush them so he could hear himself speak. And then he saw it … Peeping out of the top of the boot was something red and the red thing looked decidedly sock-ish.

'A sock,' thought the little Piglet to himself, 'is a warm thing. And warmth is just what is needed for Watching.' And with the most tremendous jump that had ever been performed by a small piglet with

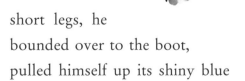

short legs, he bounded over to the boot, pulled himself up its shiny blue side and settled himself snuggly in the sock. Piglet just had time to wonder if Christopher Robin had had a bath recently and if so, if he had cleaned all his toes, even the little one at the end which was so easy to forget, before he fell fast asleep.

At about the same time, Pooh was settling down in his house for a little nap. His forgotten Wednesday lunch had tasted just as good a few days later and was now resting comfortably in his stomach. When Pooh woke up, goodness knows how many hours later, he tried hard to remember exactly what it was that he was supposed to be doing.

'Piglet!' he suddenly recalled and the idea of his small friend sitting alone on the frosty grass made him hurry out of his door as he had never hurried before. You couldn't call it a run as such, on account of the stoutness and Wednesday lunch, but it was certainly a sort of jog, a fast-ish walking kind of jog. But when Pooh arrived, there was no Piglet, and there was no boot! The winter sun was shining down on shallow water where the ice had been.

'How curious,' said Pooh to himself. 'Perhaps somebody came and took all that hard ice away and filled the place with water instead.'

Piglet woke up to the feeling of gentle rocking, which was very pleasant at first until he remembered where he was and then it became rather worrying and bothersome.

Peeping out of the boot he could see that he was bobbing along a little stream.

'Help!' he squealed and, hearing him, Pooh followed the river round a bend and then Piglet came into sight.

'Ah,' said Pooh. 'I see. Hmm …What is to be done?'

'Might a rescue be possible?' asked Piglet, hopefully. 'Of the boot, of course, but perhaps of me, too?' And, as they spoke, the boot bobbed around, occasionally turning whole circles in little eddies of water.

All this turning was making Piglet feel a little woozy in the head, but Pooh had a plan. What followed can only be described as that Brave Business of the Blue Boot. First there was a great deal of stick throwing, which caused damming, which caused boot stopping and boot wedging.

Then there was the jumping, the hopping
and the tipping. And last of all, there was
the way the news spread all through
the Forest of a Double Rescue; of
the boot and of Piglet.

The look of delight on Christopher Robin's face when
his boot was returned to him was enough to make Pooh
come over a little woozy as well. To steady himself he
made up this hum:

Walking's a perfect outside thing to do.
Climbing is fun if a friend does it too.
Stamping through long grass is better with you
And streams are made for us to splash through.

But everybody knows
When the cold gets to your toes
That the Very Best Bit of a walk or a climb,
Is being back in the warm, at about tea-time.

'Tea-time is a good idea,' said Christopher Robin.
'There's cake at my house.'

And so off they went to tea and they all lived happily ever after. THE END.

* * *

'Is that The End of the beginnings?' asked Christopher Robin, whose bath water had got cold at around the time of the flu story, so he'd got out to be sure of not catching it again. And when Pooh was climbing the Diplodocus, Christopher Robin was brushing his teeth and imagining them to be giant dinosaur jaws. Luckily, by the time they were slipping around on the ice he was tucked up in bed, which was a very good thing, because it made him shiver to even think about it.

'Thank you for helping us to remember,' said Christopher Robin, sleepily. 'Pooh had forgotten about the Brave Business of the Blue Boot,' he added, smiling to himself about all those Bs. 'Perhaps the next story can be all about Bees. Pooh would like that, especially if there was honey in it, too.' And Christopher Robin yawned and disappeared with Pooh to that warm place under the blankets where dreams are made.